Every new generation of children is enthralled by the famous stories in our Well-loved Tales series. Younger ones love to have the story read to them. Older children will enjoy the exciting stories in an easy-to-read text.

Published by Ladybird Books Ltd Loughborough Leicestershire UK
Ladybird Books Inc Lewiston Maine 04240 USA

The Enormous Turnip

retold for easy reading
by VERA SOUTHGATE, M.A., B.Com.

illustrated by CHRISTINE OWEN

Ladybird Books

Once upon a time,

in the spring,

an old man

sowed some rows of turnip seeds

in his garden.

5

As time went by,

the rain fell on the seeds

and the sun shone down on them,

and the turnips

began to grow.

7

Every day,

the turnips grew

a little bigger.

But one of them grew much faster
than all the others.

It grew large,

then very large,

then huge,

until at last it was *enormous*!

No one had ever seen

such an enormous turnip.

One day,

the old man fancied

a plateful of turnip

for his dinner.

He took off his jacket,

put on his big boots

and went out into his garden.

He gathered up the leaves

of the enormous turnip

in his two hands,

in the proper way,

and he pulled.

He pulled and pulled
with all his might,
but he could *not* pull up
the enormous turnip.

So the old man called

to his wife

to come and help to pull up

the enormous turnip.

The old woman put her arms

around her husband's waist.

Then the old man pulled

and the old woman pulled.

They pulled and pulled
with all their might,
but they could *not* pull up
the enormous turnip.

So the old woman called

to a little boy

to come and help to pull up

the enormous turnip.

They pulled and pulled
with all their might,
but they could *not* pull up
the enormous turnip.

So the old woman called

to a little boy

to come and help to pull up

the enormous turnip.

The little boy took hold

of the woman's waist.

Then the old man pulled

and the old woman pulled

and the little boy pulled.

They pulled and pulled
with all their might,
but they could *not* pull up
the enormous turnip.

So the little boy called

to a little girl

to come and help to pull up

the enormous turnip.

The little girl took hold
of the little boy's jersey.

Then the old man pulled

and the old woman pulled

and the little boy pulled

and the little girl pulled.

They pulled and pulled
with all their might,
but they could *not* pull up
the enormous turnip.

So the little girl called

to a big dog

to come and help to pull up

the enormous turnip.

The big dog took hold

of the little girl's belt.

Then the old man pulled

and the old woman pulled

and the little boy pulled

and the little girl pulled

and the big dog pulled.

They pulled and pulled
with all their might,
but they could *not* pull up
the enormous turnip.

So the big dog called

to a black cat

to come and help to pull up

the enormous turnip.

The black cat took hold

of the big dog's tail.

Then the old man pulled

and the old woman pulled

and the little boy pulled

and the little girl pulled

and the big dog pulled

and the black cat pulled.

They pulled and pulled

with all their might,

but they could *not* pull up

the enormous turnip.

The black cat called

    to a tiny mouse

    to come and help to pull up

    the enormous turnip.

The tiny mouse took hold

    of the black cat's tail.

Then the old man pulled

and the old woman pulled

and the little boy pulled

and the little girl pulled

and the big dog pulled

and the black cat pulled

and the tiny mouse pulled.

They pulled and pulled
with all their might.

And this time

they *did* pull up

the enormous turnip!

It came up with such a jerk

that they all fell down

flat on their backs.

The enormous turnip fell

on top of the old man.

The old man fell

on top of the old woman.

The old woman fell

on top of the little boy.

The little boy fell

on top of the little girl.

The little girl fell

on top of the big dog.

The big dog fell

on top of the black cat.

The black cat fell

on top of the tiny mouse.

43

After a moment,

they all jumped up,

shook themselves

and started to laugh.

They laughed and laughed

for a long, long time.

Then they carried

the enormous turnip

into the old woman's kitchen.

The old woman

cut up the turnip

and cooked it for dinner.

Then the old man

and the old woman

and the little boy

and the little girl

and the big dog

and the black cat

and the tiny mouse

all had turnip for dinner.

They all ate and ate
until they were full.
But they could not eat all
of the enormous turnip.

There was plenty of it left
for dinner the next day
and the day after.

And that was the end

of the enormous turnip.